The All Aboard Reading series is especial
by noted authors and illustrated in full cc
want to read—books to excite their imagination, expand their interests, make them
laugh, and support their feelings. With fiction and nonfiction stories that are high
interest and curriculum-related, All Aboard Reading books offer something for
every young reader. And with four different reading levels, the All Aboard Reading
series lets you choose which books are most appropriate for your children and their
growing abilities.

## Picture Readers
Picture Readers have super-simple texts, with many nouns appearing as rebus
pictures. At the end of each book are 24 flash cards—on one side is a rebus
picture; on the other side is the written-out word.

## Station Stop 1
Station Stop 1 books are best for children who have just begun to read. Simple words
and big type make these early reading experiences more comfortable. Picture clues
help children to figure out the words on the page. Lots of repetition throughout the
text helps children to predict the next word or phrase—an essential step in developing
word recognition.

## Station Stop 2
Station Stop 2 books are written specifically for children who are reading with help.
Short sentences make it easier for early readers to understand what they are reading.
Simple plots and simple dialogue help children with reading comprehension.

## Station Stop 3
Station Stop 3 books are perfect for children who are reading alone. With longer
text and harder words, these books appeal to children who have mastered basic
reading skills. More complex stories captivate children who are ready for more
challenging books.

In addition to All Aboard Reading books, look for All Aboard Math Readers™ (fiction
stories that teach math concepts children are learning in school); All Aboard Science
Readers™ (nonfiction books that explore the most fascinating science topics in
age-appropriate language); All Aboard Poetry Readers™ (funny, rhyming poems
for readers of all levels); and All Aboard Mystery Readers™ (puzzling tales where
children piece together evidence with the characters).

All Aboard for happy reading!

GROSSET & DUNLAP
Published by the Penguin Group
Penguin Group (USA) Inc., 375 Hudson Street, New York, New York 10014, U.S.A.
Penguin Group (Canada), 90 Eglinton Avenue East, Suite 700, Toronto, Ontario, Canada M4P 2Y3
(a division of Pearson Penguin Canada Inc.)
Penguin Books Ltd, 80 Strand, London WC2R 0RL, England
Penguin Ireland, 25 St Stephen's Green, Dublin 2, Ireland
(a division of Penguin Books Ltd)
Penguin Group (Australia), 250 Camberwell Road, Camberwell, Victoria 3124, Australia
(a division of Pearson Australia Group Pty Ltd)
Penguin Books India Pvt Ltd, 11 Community Centre, Panchsheel Park, New Delhi - 110 017, India
Penguin Group (NZ), Cnr Airborne and Rosedale Roads, Albany, Auckland 1310, New Zealand
(a division of Pearson New Zealand Ltd)
Penguin Books (South Africa) (Pty) Ltd, 24 Sturdee Avenue, Rosebank,
Johannesburg 2196, South Africa

Penguin Books Ltd, Registered Offices:
80 Strand, London WC2R 0RL, England

Produced by Brainwaves Limited.

ISBN 0-448-44407-0     10 9 8 7 6 5 4 3 2 1

puppy
**Scooby-Doo**™

# TIME TO PLAY

By Siobhan Ciminera and Keith Faulkner
Illustrated by Manhar Chauhan

Grosset & Dunlap

The  is shining.

There are no

in the  .

Today  will play

outside with his

new red  .

chases his

through the  and  .

The  rolls fast and far.

 is very happy.

He wiggles his little

and his little  .

The  bounces

very high—

higher than the ,

higher than the .

Even higher than the !

 wiggles his

and twitches his .

He likes his new .

's friends come over.

They like his new  .

"Can we play?" they ask.

 shakes his head.

He does not want

to share his new  !

"See how fast my new

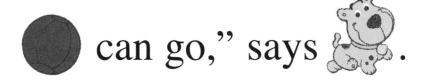 can go," says  .

The  rolls too fast

down the

to the mud.

It is going to land

in the  !

"Don't worry," says  .

"See how far my

can go," says  .

He kicks the

too hard.

It lands in the

with a  .

"Don't worry," say

and  .

"See how high my 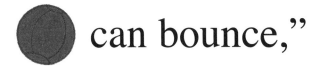 can bounce,"

says  .

But the 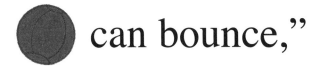 bounces

too high and gets stuck

in a 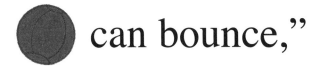 .

"Don't worry," says  .

"Let me bounce the

again," says  .

This time the

bounces too far.

"Don't worry," says

as she lifts  over the

 by his  .

"Everyone helped me

get my  back,"

says  .

"Thank you so much."

 knows it's not fun

playing with his

new  alone.

"Would everyone

still like to play

with me?"  asks.

"Yes," says  .

Everyone agrees.

 and his friends

play with the red

for the rest of the day.

They all have so much fun

playing together.

| clouds | sun |
| --- | --- |
| Puppy Scooby-Doo | sky |
| grass | ball |

| tail | flowers |
|------|---------|
| bush | ears |
| tree | doghouse |

| hill | nose |
|------|------|
| Kate | mud |
| splash | pond |

| | |
|---|---|
| Max | Lily |
| fence | Twizz |
| collar | Laurabel |